William John Lawson

A Handy Book on the Law of Banking

SALZWASSER
VERLAG

William John Lawson

A Handy Book on the Law of Banking

Reprint of the original, first published in 1859.

1st Edition 2022 | ISBN: 978-3-37512-256-0

Verlag (Publisher): Salzwasser Verlag GmbH, Zeilweg 44, 60439 Frankfurt, Deutschland
Vertretungsberechtigt (Authorized to represent): E. Roepke, Zeilweg 44, 60439 Frankfurt, Deutschland
Druck (Print): Books on Demand GmbH, In de Tarpen 42, 22848 Norderstedt, Deutschland

[ENTERED AT STATIONERS' HALL.]

A

HANDY BOOK

ON

THE LAW OF BANKING:

WITH A CLEAR AND COMPLETE EXPOSITION OF

ITS PRINCIPLES, CUSTOMS, AND PRACTICE,

IN

ENGLAND, SCOTLAND, AND IRELAND.

BY

WILLIAM JOHN LAWSON,

AUTHOR OF "THE HISTORY OF BANKING."

"Laws ought not to be subtle, since they are designed for people of common understanding."—MONTESQUIEU.

THIRD THOUSAND.

London:

EFFINGHAM WILSON, ROYAL EXCHANGE.

1859.

PREFACE.

HAVING had upwards of thirty years' experience of the law and practice of banking, I feel myself justified in having undertaken the compilation of the following treatise.

Much of the law of banking is the result of such cases as have, from time to time, been decided in our courts. It is thus greatly a matter of prece-dent. All such works, however, as contain what may be termed the written laws, have been carefully consulted and condensed.

My endeavour has been to embrace the legal re-sults of as many decisions as I could consistently with the desire of bringing the work within the compass of what its title imports.

WILLIAM JOHN LAWSON.

CONTENTS.

CHAPTER I.

INTRODUCTION.

1. *How Corporations may be established.*
2. *How Charters are distinguished from Acts of Parliament.*
3. *By whom Charters are granted, and how.*
4. *Difference between Incorporated and Unincorporated Bodies.*

1. As all future banks of more than six partners must be established by letters patent or by Royal Charter, we propose to glance cursorily at the nature of charters, and then consider the peculiar laws, principles, customs, and practices of the existing banks, in the United Kingdom.

When a body of men become incorporated by Royal Charter or letters patent, they are termed bodies politic or corporate, and they may be established in three different ways, viz., by prescription, by letters patent, or by Act of Parliament, but most generally by patent or charter. The City of London is a corporation by prescription.

When a corporation is lawfully created, all powers, such as to purchase and grant, sue and be sued, are tacitly annexed to the Charter; and although no powers to make laws, statutes, or ordinances, are given by a special clause to a corporation, they are included by law, in the very act of incorporation, as without such powers the charter would be inoperative.

2. Charters are distinguished from Acts of Parliament in this way, viz., that the former are writings sealed with the Great Seal of England, by virtue of which, a body of men are authorised to do or to enjoy anything exclusively for a period of time named in the Charter, and which of themselves, singly or collectively, they are unable to do.

3. The privilege of granting charters is the exclusive prerogative of the Crown, and they are usually stated to be granted by " virtue of the King's prerogative Royal, and of his especial grace, certain knowledge, and mere motion."

Letters patent or Charters are so called by reason of the form, as being open with the seal affixed, ready to be shown for the confirmation of the authority thereby given; but in the case of an incorporated body constituted by Act of Parliament, there is nothing to show save a printed statement of the proceedings of the Houses of Parliament on a given day, which statement is called an Act of Parliament, and usually begins thus: " Be it enacted by the Queen's most excellent Majesty, by and with the advice and consent of the Lords Spiritual and Temporal, and Commons in this present Parliament assembled, and by the authority of the same;" and so forth.

Thus for instance the Bank of England was established conjointly by an Act of Parliament and Royal Charter; its common seal is and must be affixed, to every bank note that is issued, and consists of the not very handsome representation of Britannia. The Bank of Scotland was incorporated by an Act of the Scottish Parliament, and the Bank of Ireland by the Irish Parliament; the two latter have, therefore, no written authority.

Royal Charters, for the formation of banking establishments, were seldom granted; we had until recently only one in England—the Bank of England; and in Scotland four—the Royal Bank, the British Linen Company, the National Bank, and the Commercial Bank of Scotland. In Ireland there are none.

4. In an incorporated bank, the law does not recognise individuals, but knows it only in its corporate character; for a corporation being an invisible body cannot manifest its intentions by any personal act or oral discourse; it is said to have no soul or conscience, but acts and speaks only by its common seal. In an unincorporated body, on the contrary, the law recognises individuals only in their character as co-partners in the undertaking.

The following are some of the legal advantages of an incorporated over an unincorporated bank. No creditor can attach any shareholder without first seeking his remedy against the corporate funds and property of the bank, which must first be exhausted before any legal proceedings can be taken against an individual shareholder, and not then without special application to a judge, and even in that case the law provides a remedy, for every shareholder must contribute an equitable proportion to protect the party who may be sued.

Nor can the losses of the corporation be unjustly entailed upon any single member of the body Corporate, but must be distributed over the whole of the members in proportion to the number of shares held by them respectively.

When a charter is put an end to by the parties themselves it is said to have committed suicide.

CHAPTER II.

OF THE POWERS, PRIVILEGES, AND ADVANTAGES OF THE CORPORATION OF THE BANK OF ENGLAND.

1. *Powers granted by the Charter.*
2. *On the privilege of its being Bankers to the State.*
3. *Nature of its business with the Government, and the legal safeguards that surround it:*
4. *The separation of the Bank into two independent Departments, one for the issue of Notes and the other for Banking purposes. Legal effects of this measure.*
5. *Regulation as to the public Accounts.*
6. *Its Agency business.*

1. In giving a digest of the laws and customs relating to banking, it must be evident that the Bank of England claims our first consideration; for history furnishes no example that can at all be compared with it, for the range and multiplicity of its transactions, and for the vast influence it possesses over public and national affairs.

The charter of this important corporation, which is in force at the present day, was granted in 1694, by William and Mary. It enumerates at some length the fundamental principles of the corporation, and displays, in the manner in which it is drawn up, a considerable extent of knowledge of commercial affairs.

It restricts the corporation to the dealing in bills of exchange, and in gold and silver. It prohibits its members, as a body, from taking part in any mercantile concern, but authorises them to make advances of money on the security of merchandise lodged with it, or pledged by written documents. It also provides for the manner in which such pledged goods may be disposed of, in case of non-redemption.

The privileges conferred by this charter have from time to time been made the subject of parliamentary inquiries, on which several laws have been founded, but without in any way disturbing the fundamental principles of the constitution of the bank.

The charter makes no reference to the limitation of the liability of the stockholders of the bank, but the Act of Parliament, on which the charter is based, provides that the corporation shall not at any time borrow more than the amount of the capital of the bank, unless authorised by Parliament to do so; and if any further sum is borrowed under the common seal of the bank, "each member of the corporation, in his and their respective capacities, shall be chargeable with and liable, in proportion, to their several shares and subscriptions, to the repayment of the money borrowed." This clause, it is considered, limits the liability of the stockholders.

2. The Governor and Company of the Bank of England are constituted by Act of Parliament bankers to the State, and book-keepers in respect to the National Debt, created from time to time by the legislature. It is a duty they owe to all persons who may be interested in the purchase or sale of the public funds, so to keep the accounts as that it may distinctly appear, at all times, what transfers and assignments have been made.

3. It is felony for any person wilfully to make any false entry, or alter any words or figures, in any of the books of accounts in which any stock, annuities, or public funds are kept, with intent to defraud any person whatever.

The transfer of stock in the public funds is further guarded by making it felony to forge such transfers, or to forge a power of attorney to transfer or to receive dividends thereon, or to effect a transfer or receive dividends on any of the public funds by false personation.

The nature of stock and money in the public funds is this: Stock is a chose in action; it has no locality, except for the purposes of probate and administration; it does not fall under the head of goods and chattels; it cannot be sued for as money; it does not pass under the term "money" in a will, but it does pass under the term "securities for money," unless the expression be controlled by the context. However, stock in the funds has been said to pass or not under the word "monies," or the word "goods" or "chattels," according to the whole

1 §

context of the will ; and either "goods" or "chattels," used simply and without qualification, will pass it in a will; and when a testator did not bank with the Bank of England, "a bequest of all my money in the Bank of England" passed as money in the funds. There are numerous cases to be found in our law records establishing the above doctrine.

The stock-books of the bank cannot be inspected by persons who have no interest therein, or who may seek inspection for the purpose of a private nature unconnected with the objects for which the books are kept.

A fundholder has a right to inspect and copy entries relating to the stock and its transfers, &c., in which he is personally interested; but he has only the right as to particular entries, relating to a certain parcel of stock, and no other, and only then by being able to furnish a list of such bank-books as contain entries of stock in which the party applying is concerned.

To show the importance of transacting the business of the National Debt, it is only necessary to state that the debt amounts to £735,000,000, which amount is divisible into any number of accounts, with only one limit—that no one is allowed to have a smaller account than the value of one penny.

The number of accounts opened at the present time is 270,000, and for every account an order, or what is called a warrant, is made out every half-year, for the payment of dividends, from each of which a separate deduction has to be made for income-tax, which latter the bank pays over to the Government in one gross sum at each half-yearly payment of dividends.

The title to every particle of stock is given on the responsibility of the bank, and although the stock may have been transferred, under a forged power of attorney, no question can ever arise affecting the right or title of the holder when once the stock has passed into his name.*

Since the passing of the Act 4 and 5 Will. IV, cap. 15, which remodelled the Exchequer, and provided that all the future payments on account of the public revenue should be made to the Bank of England direct, the

* Thomson Hankey, 'Lecture on Banking.'

arrangements for public payments have been greatly simplified. They are now made by drafts of the Paymaster-General on the bank, many of which pass into bankers' hands, and are adjusted by simple transfers to their accounts with the bank.

The agency of the bank is also employed with great advantage in the receipt of the public revenues. Wherever there is a branch of that establishment, a clerk attends the Collector of the Inland Revenue on his rounds, and carries the money received to public account. The next day credit is given for it in the Exchequer account with the bank in London.

The branches of the bank established at the most considerable ports are in like manner made available for the remittance of Custom duties, which are daily paid in to them by the collectors, and credited to the public in London.

The risk, delay, and expense of transmitting public monies to London through other channels are avoided, by these simple arrangements, and temptations to fraud are almost, if not entirely, removed.

These facilities and advantages are derived from the employment by the Government of a central establishment, connected with the general body of bankers, and having branches of its own in different parts of the country.

These advantages are further developed by the monetary transactions that banks and corporations have with the Bank of England, and which facilitate the arrangements with respect to the dividends which the former are entitled to receive. They are paid by carrying the dividend warrants to their credit in their accounts with the bank.

The dividends paid each quarter amount to about £5,800,000. Of this sum about £3,800,000 is transferred to the accounts of different corporations and banks by a mere stroke of the pen, in a few hours, and all the labour which would attend the issue of notes for that large amount is saved.

The beneficial effects of this arrangement, at critical periods, can hardly be over-estimated. The invariable and regular payment of the interest on public debts provides not only a useful employment for every man's money, but each individual has also an advantage in the support given to that State of which he is a member; because, in granting it, he exonerates himself from further evils to which he would be exposed if the State refused or was unable to pay.

4. The last Bank Act made it compulsory on the Bank of England to divide their establishment, exclusive of the Government department, into two wholly distinct departments, one to be called the Issue Department, and the other the Banking Department.

To effect this object, the bank found it necessary to transfer to the issue department securities to the value of £14,000,000, of which a debt due by the Government, amounting to £11,000,000, formed a part. At the same time there was transferred to the issue department so much of the gold and silver then held by the bank as, together with the above £14,000,000, would equal the amount of notes then in circulation. No notes to be henceforth issued except in exchange for other notes, or on receipt of gold coin or bullion; but the £14,000,000 of notes are permitted to circulate without any other security than the Government stock held by the bank.

The banking department is authorised to make payments in and issue such bank notes as may be received from the issue department.

All persons may demand of the issue department notes in exchange for gold bullion, at the rate of £3 17s. 9d. per ounce of standard gold; and the bank is compelled to purchase all gold at that price, regardless of the amount offered to them, and in return for which they are to give bank notes, and for which gold, they receive from the Mint coins at the rate of £3 17s. 10½d. per ounce. The small difference, viz., 1½d. per ounce, between the Mint and the bank price of gold, constitutes a charge on the owner of bullion which is perhaps not more than that which he would incur in preparing for coinage, and in the loss of interest on his treasure while detained at the Mint. In this, as in other branches of industry, the advantage of the division of labour is apparent. The importer of gold dust takes it to the refiner, the refiner delivers it to the Bank of England, and the bank transfers it to the Mint for coinage when necessary. All three obtain their profit from the arrangement; the first two from the speedy payment in money ; the bank from the profit on the coinage.

Should the notes issued by the bank, on securities, at any time and under any circumstances exceed the limited amount of £14,000,000, the profit derived from such over-issue, after deducting the expenses incurred, consequent on such additional issue, are to be deducted from the amount payable to the bank for charges of management of the public debts. And in consideration of the exclusive privileges of banking which the Act confers on the corporation, and the exemption from stamp-duty on their notes, the bank are further to deduct from the said charges of management the annual sum of £180,000.

5. The Bank of England is also a bank of deposit, loan, and discount ; but, unlike other joint-stock banks, it does not issue any circular notes, or grant letters of credit on foreign countries. It does not allow interest to its depositors, be the amount ever so large. Neither are the customers of the bank allowed, on any consideration, to overdraw their accounts. In discounting bills the tariff of rates differs according to the nature of the securities tendered, but the bank never charge less than the minimum rate publicly announced.

6. The London agency business of the Bank of Ireland and the Royal Bank of Scotland are the only country banks with which the Bank of England does business ; all bills drawn by these two banks are drawn " without acceptance."

In addition to the issue of notes, as before referred to, the Bank of England issues bank post bills, at seven days' sight ; and for the convenience of remittance to India bank post bills, at sixty days' sight, are issued, which, being accepted at the time they are drawn, the sixty days begin to run from the date, so that the bills are payable immediately on their return to London from India.

This advantage, and the unquestionable credit of the paper, often enables the holder in India to dispose of them at a good premium in the India market, in certain states of the exchanges, and thus they become as it were an article of commerce. The practice of issuing bank post bills does not extend to the branches of the bank.

CHAPTER III.

OF THE NATURE AND QUALITY OF BANK OF ENGLAND NOTES.

1. *The legal definition of Bank Notes.*
2. *Practice of the Bank in respect to lost notes.*
3. *Bank never re-issue their notes; advantages of this practice.*
4. *Where and how Bank Notes are to be made payable.*
5. *On the legal tender of Bank Notes.*
6. *The Bank refuse to discount for Bill-brokers; effects of the measure.*
7. *Custom of the Bank in respect to the bills they discount.*
8. *Publication of assets and liabilities by the Bank.*
9. *Numerous Acts of Parliament in relation to the Bank.*
10. *When the powers granted to the Corporation are to cease.*
11. *Library in the Bank for the use of the clerks.*

1. Bank of England notes, unlike other choses in action, are capable of acquiring a locality; and were considered to be so, previously to their being made a legal tender, &c.; in short, they have always been held to pass in a will by a bequest of all the testator should have in his house at his death, or equivalent terms. But it is not so in the case of country bank notes, any such notes that may be in the house would not pass under such words.

2. As a matter of course the Bank of England always receive value in one shape or another for every note they issue, the notes are consequently payable to bearer on demand; the payment of them by the Bank of England, on presentation, is therefore imperative.

When notes have been lost or stolen, it is customary to give notice to the Bank of such loss, with particulars of the amount, number and date of each note, which notice the Bank enter in a book, and for which they charge a small fee.

This is commonly called "stopping payment of a note," but for reasons above stated, all that the Bank can legally do when a note, which they have received notice has been lost, &c., is presented for payment, is to inform the party who gave the notice that the note has been presented through such and such a bank.

If tendered to the Bank by a stranger who, on inquiry, proves to be a *bonâ fide* holder and owner of the note, the authorities of the Bank intimate, in a respectful manner, that the note has been stopped, requesting him to wait until an opportunity is afforded to the party who stopped it to inspect the note, &c.; a special messenger is immediately dispatched with the information of the presentation of the note, and if the party does not attend within a reasonable time the note is paid : any unnecessary delay or offensive detention of the person presenting the note would subject the Bank to an action for false imprisonment.

There are occasions, however, when the Bank do absolutely stop the payment of their notes, but this is not done without the Bank being guaranteed against the consequences thereof; so that if a note, on which a stop has been placed, is presented by a *bonâ fide* holder, and is refused, and an action against the Bank for the recovery of the amount of the note is the result of such refusal, the Bank are of course indemnified.

The consequences likely to result from the absolute stopping the payment of Bank of England notes are of too serious a character to be disregarded, especially in respect of notes transmitted from abroad, for bank notes pass freely on the Continent among bankers and exchange brokers, who readily deal in them.

On a recent occasion the Bank stopped two of their notes for £500 each, which notes had been exchanged by two Paris bankers in the ordinary course of their business, and transmitted to their London agents : on the refusal of payment two actions were brought against the Bank. Although in both cases the facts were almost identical, yet in the one case the plaintiff recovered, and in the other the jury decided in favour of the Bank. The action in the latter case was subsequently compromised, but not till after the parties had incurred enormous expenses in law proceedings.

When the result of these actions became known in Paris all the bankers affixed notices, in a conspicuous part of the office, to the effect that no Bank of England notes would, for the future, be exchanged by that bank, thus throwing a discredit on Bank of England notes.

Such stoppage of the payment of bank notes might give rise to another serious annoyance to the Bank. A note so stopped could be protested for non-payment, and, if of sufficient amount, notice of bankruptcy might be served on the Bank, a result which some years ago absolutely took place in respect to a note of the Bank of Ireland.

3. The Bank never re-issue their notes; when once tendered for payment they are destroyed; the process of destroying the notes is by burning them, but this operation does not take place till they have been laid aside for a given number of years. The whole are not destroyed together, but at different times, and as many are burnt as correspond with the new notes issued.

The Bank of England at one time tried the experiment of re-issuing their notes, but were obliged to return to the former practice; the innovation interfered with the simplicity of the registration system. The expense and trouble of fabricating notes was found to be inconsiderable when compared with the delay and risk which attended the counting and recording notes not bearing consecutive numbers. The system now in force must therefore be considered as identical with the business habits of the community, and any change which would impair its efficiency or clog the wheels by which money transactions are carried on with the rapidity, regularity and security, observable in a London bank, would be regarded as a serious evil.

4. All promissory notes of the Bank, payable on demand, must be made payable at the place where issued; it is not lawful for the Bank, or for any person on its behalf, to issue, at any place out of London, any such notes, not made payable at the place where the same is issued.

Although Bank of England notes are a legal tender

at all places, except the Bank itself, yet practically they are not a legal tender in the banking department of the Bank; for instance, let any one present a £500 note at the latter department, and demand gold for it, he would be told that he must present the note at the only place where it is payable in gold, viz., the issue department.

There are some curious anomalies in the important matter of the legal tender which seem to require attention. Thus, in England, gold or Bank of England notes will discharge a debt. In Scotland and Ireland nothing but gold is a legal tender to discharge a debt.

6. The Bank of England were accustomed for many years to grant accommodation, in the way of discounts, to bill-brokers; now, however, they have declined doing business with them, the object being to keep the resources of the Bank more under control. The immense drain upon the Bank, which so frequently took place, proved the necessity for a change.

7. It is a custom with the Bank of England, in reference to the bills they discount, that if the acceptors to any such bills become insolvent or bankrupt before the bills become due, to call upon the parties for whom they were discounted to withdraw them, without waiting till they are matured; and, however inconvenient this might be, the bills must be at once taken out of the hands of the Bank, otherwise no further accommodation, in the shape of discounts, will be afforded to the party failing to do so.

8. The Bank are to furnish, for publication in the *Gazette*, a weekly statement of the amount of notes issued by the issue department, together with the amount of gold coin and bullion, as well as securities held against such notes; also a separate account from the banking department of the capital stock, and the deposits, and of the money and securities belonging to the Bank.

9. There are numerous Acts of Parliament, more or less connected with the Bank, relating to advances to Government, the purchase of Government securities, the public balances in the hands of the Bank, restrictions on and resumption of cash payments, restraining the negotiation of promissory notes under a limited sum, the circulation of silver tokens, the protection of the

property of the Bank, the punishment of persons guilty of forging their notes, and counterfeiting tokens; and regulating modes of transacting business with the Bank in relation to public accounts, directed to be opened there for greater security, &c. The Acts are stated in an abbreviated form, in the general collection of the statutes, the mere titles of which extend to nearly 200 pages.

10. In accordance with these Acts the Bank of England is to enjoy the exclusive privilege of banking, and all other powers given or recognised as belonging to or enjoyed by the Bank, until the repayment by parliament of the sum of £11,000,000, being the amount of the Government debt due to the Bank, without any deduction or abatement whatever, and upon payment to the Bank of all arrears of £100,000 per annum, together with the interest or annuity payable on the debt due to the Bank, and also upon the repayment of all the principal and interest on every description of public securities held by the Bank, then and in that case, and not till then, the exclusive privilege of banking, granted to the Corporation, shall cease and determine.

11. Although the following account may not, strictly speaking, fall within the range of subjects marked out for this work, yet we think the record of such an event here may be pardoned.

Many of the clerks of the Bank of England expressed a desire to form a library and literary institution within the walls of the Bank; a set of rules and regulations were drawn up, subject to the approval of the Governor and Deputy-Governor.

Not only were these rules and regulations cordially approved of, but the court of directors appropriated and fitted up, at a considerable expense, a large room as a library; and, in addition, presented the committee of management with books to the value of £500, leaving the entire future arrangement and management of the library in the hands of the members of the institution.

We think this one of the most important steps in connexion with the internal government of the Bank that has ever yet been taken; it shows a great desire on the part of the directors to do all in their power to relieve the monotony of the duties of the officials in the Bank, whilst at the same time it reflects the greatest credit on the promoters and committee of management for their exertions in furnishing their fellow-clerks, especially the younger men, with the means of adding to their moral and intellectual improvement.

CHAPTER IV.

LAWS, CUSTOMS, AND PRACTICES OF BANKS NOT BEING BANKS OF ISSUE.

1. *Of the nature and business of Bankers.*
2. *Bankers are bound to obey the orders of their customers. Serious consequences which may result from their neglecting to do so.*
3. *The Statute of Limitation when applicable to Bankers.*
4. *A Banker must know his customer's hand-writing.*
5. *On the duties of a Banker in reference to bills for acceptance, and the law respecting non-accepted bills.*
6. *On the liability of a Banker receiving money lodged with him for an illegal purpose.*
7. *On the liability of Bankers paying cheques for a customer after his Bankruptcy.*
8. *Definition of the term " Money at call."*
9. *The nature of short bills ; how far a Banker may be considered as acting illegally in disposing of them.*
10. *Lien by Bankers, part of the " law merchant."*
11. *On Guarantees given to Bankers.*
12. *On Guarantees given by Bankers.*
13. *Bankers' books, on the legal importance of their being correctly kept.*
14. *On the legal importance of Bankers' pass books.*
15. *Difference between money of a customer in the hands of his Banker, and money in his own hands.*
16. *Difference between Banks of deposit which do not issue notes, and Banks of issue.*
17. *Legislating for non-issuing private Banks not necessary.*

1. The nature of the business of banking has been laid down by very high authority to be part of the " law merchant ;" it principally consists in borrowing money or receiving money at interest, as well as lending upon securities, bankers thereby form a connecting link in the chain between the operative and inoperative classes, they

become the debtors of the capitalists and the creditors of the producers or distributors of revenue, and thus afford a ready medium of adjustment between the interests of these two great divisions of society.

It is therefore the chief object of a banker's study, and his constant desire, to search out and make choice of, the most secure as well as the most profitable subject for the employment of the capital placed under his charge, and for the safety of which he is responsible.

The business of banking as distinguished from mercantile business is, that the one is a dealer in money and credit, and the other in produce; each may be carried on purely as a commission business. The merchant sells goods on commission, the banker may be said to sell credit; he, however, charges no commission, but is satisfied on receiving a certain per-centage for the use of his money, and his customer readily pays the charge, which is sometimes called interest, and at other times discount; the latter term with bankers has another signification, for it is also applied to parties who cannot obtain accomodation on the ordinary terms, and whose credit is consequently said to be at a *discount*.

A banker, in his character as a dealer in money, is purely an agent, for he undertakes to dispose of the monies lodged in his hands by his customers in any way and in any sum, that they his customers may in their discretion think fit to order, not exceeding the amount standing to their credit; as an agent, therefore, the banker should be paid.

2. Bankers are bound to obey the orders of their customers within the usual course of business; if they disobey them they are responsible both for the delay and any consequences which directly follow the delay; for instance, a banker in the country instructs his London banker to pay to a life assurance company, on a given day, a certain sum as the annual premium on a policy of assurance on the life of A. B. Should the banker neglect to pay the same, after consenting to do so, he would be liable, in the event of the death of A. B., to pay the amount of the sum assured.

Although, in general, bankers are bound to comply with the orders of their customers, yet they may refuse, and by that means relieve themselves from all responsibility to the persons in whose favour the order is made.

When a banker receives instructions to invest money deposited in his hands by a customer in any specific manner, and assents, or does not repudiate the order, he is in the situation of a trustee or agent with reference to that money.

When a customer pays to his banker a sum of money, and, at the time of doing so, gives written instructions that the money is for the express purpose of providing for particular bills, and the banker, instead of following his instructions, places the amount to the credit of his general account, which at the time is overdrawn, and the bills are consequently dishonoured; should the bankruptcy of the customer follow, his assignees can recover the whole of the sum from the bankers, who would also be liable to an action for the consequences of the non-performance of the instructions of the customer, on which, by receiving the money, they tacitly consented to act.

By the 7 and 8 Geo. IV, cap. 29, bankers may, under certain circumstances, render themselves liable to transportation by misapplying securities entrusted to them.

The following is the clause for the punishment of agents intrusted with property :

"That if any money or security for the payment of money shall be entrusted to any banker, merchant, broker, attorney, or other agent, *with any direction in writing*, to apply such money or any part thereof, or the proceeds, or any part of the proceeds, of such security, for any purpose specified in such direction, and he shall, in violation of good faith, and contrary to the purpose so specified, in any wise convert to his own use or benefit, such money, &c., and being convicted thereof, shall be liable at the discretion of the court to be transported beyond the seas for any term not exceeding fourteen years nor less than seven."

The above act has been further strengthened by the following :

"If any banker intrusted with the property of any other person for safe custody, shall, with intent to defraud, sell, negotiate, transfer, pledge, or in any other manner convert or appropriate property so intrusted to his care, to or for his own use, or any part thereof, will be guilty of a misdemeanor.

"If any director, member, or public officer of any public company shall fraudulently take or apply to his own use any of the money or property of such company, will be guilty of misdemeanor.

"If any director, manager, or public officer of any public company, shall as such, fraudulently appropriate property, or keep fraudulent accounts, wilfully destroy books, or publish fraudulent statements of accounts, knowing them to be false in any material particular, with intent to deceive or defraud, will be guilty of a misdemeanor."

3. Money paid in to a banker is a borrowing on the part of the banker, and a lending on the part of the customer.

The statute of limitation runs against such debts as against any other simple contract debt, and, consequently, bankers, with whom money has been deposited, might insist, if there had been no other transaction between them, that they never promised to pay the balance within six years, and that would be a good defence in law—as to the wisdom of such a defence no comment is necessary.

Where a banker is made a trustee, and funds are allowed to remain in his hands for upwards of six years, and when after that period application is made by the party beneficially interested in such funds, the statute of limitation will not apply.

4. The proposition has been laid down more than once, that it is part of the duty of a banker to his customer, to be well acquainted with his customer's handwriting; it has even been said that he is bound not only to know his customer's hand-writing, but also what is not his hand-writing; and if he pays an order which afterwards proves to have been forged, he must bear the loss; this renders it necessary for a banker to exercise the utmost caution in discharging the obligations of his customers.

A bill purporting to have been accepted by a customer payable at his bankers, was presented and paid. The banker, on *the following day*, discovered the acceptance to have been a forgery and demanded back the money.

The court held that the holder was entitled to know on the day the bill became due, that it was a forgery; the banker could, therefore, not recover.

5. When a banker receives a bill from a customer with instructions to get it accepted, and acceptance is refused, and the banker omits to give notice of non-acceptance, the depositor has a right of action against him, and may recover damages in proportion to the injury he may have sustained, even to the full amount of the bill.

The non-acceptance of a bill of exchange on presentation is the dishonour of the bill; and when due notice of such refusal to accept is given to the parties interested in the bill, and, in case of its being a foreign bill, a protest for non-acceptance is forwarded, it is not obligatory on a banker to present it again, even for payment, when it purports to be due.

It has been decided in cases of this kind, that if a bill which is given in payment does not turn out to be productive in consequence of non-acceptance, it is not that which it purported to be, or that which the party receiving it in discharge of a debt expected, and, therefore, he may consider it as a nullity, and act as if no such bill had been given.

6. Bankers are not unfrequently liable to be made responsible for the objects of those who lodge sums of money with them, to be retained and paid over on a given event. Thus, a banker, who permits a sum of money to be paid into his bank for the purpose of being paid over, for corruptly procuring an appointment under government, may be indicted for a conspiracy, along with those who are to procure the appointment and to receive the money.*

7. If bankers receive and pay money on account of a bankrupt, after notice of his bankruptcy, they cannot set off the payments against the receipts, for, as every one is bound to know the law, they must be considered to have known that a bankrupt was not a free agent, and has no longer the disposition of his property; that by honouring his cheques they performed an illegal act, and the assignees would be entitled to recover the whole of the sums received, without any deduction for the payments, whatever their amount may be.

* R. v. Pollman, 2 Camb. 233.

8. Some bankers open what is called a deposit account with any customer who desires to deal in that manner; that is to say, the customer deposits a sum, on which the banker agrees to pay a certain fixed rate of interest, and which may be entirely withdrawn at any time by the depositor, without notice, on presenting the receipt with his name endorsed on it, when the principal with interest upon it to the day of payment is handed to him.

It has of late years been the practice of bankers, both public and private, who have a redundancy of capital, to employ large sums at call, that is, lending it to bill-brokers with the option of having it back at any moment, the latter employ it in discounts.

But the lending money to bill-brokers upon the security of bills deposited with the bank, is not discounting—for discounting bills and lending money on bills are two very distinct operations.

When bills are discounted, they are the property of the bank, but when brokers borrow money on the deposit of bills, the bankers lending the money are not justified in considering such bills in any other light than a mortgage, to be returnable intact when the money borrowed on them is repaid.

Bankers generally regard money left with brokers, on call, as one of the most immediately available assets which they have to meet their liabilities; but it does sometimes happen, in times of panic, that money on call with brokers does not come when it is asked for, in consequence of the brokers being themselves in difficulties. Money on deposit at bankers may be said to be money at call, for they do not require any notice of withdrawal, there being a constant circulation of persons every day, some paying in money and some withdrawing it; but there is this difference between money at call with a joint-stock bank, and money at call with bill-brokers; in the former case no interest is allowed on deposits unless they remain with the bank at least one month; in the latter, a small per-centage is allowed.

The rate of interest allowed on money at call is usually a shade lower than money deposited for a certain term, let that term be ever so short.

9. The term "short bills," and entering "bills short," are frequently met with in cases relating to the law of banking. Such bills, in the absence of special agreement between the parties to the contrary, or habits of dealing from which such agreement may be inferred, are considered in the nature of a deposit; the property in them is not changed on the bankruptcy of the banker, with such bills in his possession. They may be recovered.

Where bills deposited with a banker are endorsed by the party depositing them, the clearly settled rule is, that if the banker negotiates them to a third party, though the purpose for which they were deposited be ever so cruelly disappointed, by the bankruptcy of the banker, the original owner who deposited them can have no claim to recover them in trover against any third party, but must come in as a general creditor of the banker.

Lord Eldon frequently declared, when sitting in Bankruptcy, that it ought to be generally known, that if bills endorsed are remitted to bankers, they may dispose of them effectually, though contrary to the faith of the understanding between the parties, and the remitters can only come in as general creditors.*

It is only when bills of exchange, or other securities, are deposited for a specific purpose with bankers, that the property remains in the depositor.

There is another class of cases where money deposited in a bank may remain the property of the depositor, and therefore recoverable.

Thus, where a person had deposited a large sum of money with a banker, after banking hours, the manager knowing that the bank was on the eve of stopping payment, though no formal resolution to that effect had been come to, lodged the money in a place by itself, separate from the funds of the bank, and the bank never after that day opened for business; it was held that the depositor was entitled to recover from the assignees. This decision has frequently been acted upon.

10. The general lien by bankers is also part of the

* Ex parte Wakefield Bank, 1 Rose, 246.

law Merchant, to be judicially noticed like other parts of the law. A banker's lien does not attach on securities placed in his hands for a special purpose. Such, for instance, as Exchequer bills, on which he is simply instructed to receive the interest, and get them paid or exchanged for other bills, as the case may be, when advertised by the Government.

Bankers have no lien for the balance of an overdrawn account against a customer on his plate deposited with them for safe custody.

Neither can bankers carry into effect any lien which they may, *prima facie*, have upon securities deposited with them, which are in fact trust-deeds. Thus, if a customer deposits title-deeds as security for an advance of money, and the property comprised in the deeds is subject to a trust, *in breach of which the deposit is made*, then, although the bankers have no notice of the trust, it must prevail against their lien.

Bankers have no lien on the deposit of a partner on his separate account for a balance due to the bank from the firm.

Little has been decided to illustrate how the law provides that the banker is to realise and make productive such securities as he may lawfully have a lien on.

In case of any negotiable security which comes to his hands on account of a customer, to whom the banker is in advance, he has a lien or power of detention, and in order to make such power productive, he may put the negotiable instrument in suit, and recover upon it so much as will cover the balance due to him from the customer.

But instead of advancing their remedy bankers will destroy their right of lien, if after a lien has been established, they take a security, *which is payable at a distant day*, for the debt.

GUARANTEES.

11. The numerous cases which have been contested in the courts of law respecting guarantees to bankers on simple contracts, and the oft-times conflicting decisions which have been pronounced on instruments very nearly approaching to identity of signification in their

terms, rendered it most unsafe for bankers to rely on merely written, not sealed and delivered guarantees.

In all guarantees given since 19 & 20, Vict., cap. 97, the necessity for the statement of consideration can be dispensed with, provided the undertaking be in writing and signed by the party to be charged therewith, or by some other party duly authorised.

12. Bankers are sometimes required to give security for one of their firm, on his being appointed treasurer or receiver to public bodies. In such cases it is an established principle that, if a person is surety for another for the due accounting for monies received by him, the receipt of monies by the partners is not the same as the receipt by him alone, because the surety may be willing to be accountable for the acts of one individual, but not for him and his partners. Hence, when a bank failed with a balance due to a public body, the sureties were held not to be liable, because A, the treasurer, never had, in fact, been in the exclusive receipt of the monies which were paid into the bank.*

13. We may observe upon the absolute necessity of keeping the books of a bank correctly; the entries in them are obviously of the greatest importance, not only to the interest of the customer, but, as we shall presently show, to the bank also, for it must be from the books alone that the clerks of the bank and others are to decide whether the cheque of a customer is to be honoured or not, and because it has been decided to be proper to receive in evidence a banker's ledger, in order to show that a customer had or had not assets on a given day in the banker's hands.

Should a cheque be presented to a banker within banking hours, and it be returned dishonoured while the drawer had sufficient funds in the hands of the bank to pay the amount drawn for, the banker would be liable to substantial damages. It will be no answer to an action of this sort that the account was wrong cast, or that the last payment made by the customer was placed to a wrong account.

* Mills *v.* Alderbury Union, 3 Exch., 590.

The correctness in book-keeping by bankers is further necessary, inasmuch as most bankers adopt the unsafe practice of returning to their customers the cheques drawn on and paid by them, so that in point of fact a banker, having parted with the only tangible document which was both his authority for paying and voucher for having done so, has no other evidence of the payments made by him for a customer, than the entries in his books.

14. Bankers are in the habit of furnishing to each customer a book, called a "pass-book," on which, at the head of the first page, and there only, the bankers are described as the debtors, and the customer as the creditor in account.

On the left-hand side of this book are entered all sums received by the bankers on account of the customer, and on the right-hand side all sums paid to him or his order, and the entries being summed up at the bottom of each page, the amounts are carried to the next page, and this operation is continued until the half-yearly period for balancing the books arrives, when the book is balanced, and the balance carried forward to the credit or debit of the bank, as the case may be, which balance must agree with the banker's ledger, of which the pass-book is considered to be a transcript.

Credit given in a pass-book binds the banker, for by entering the same to the customer's credit, they lead him to suppose that they had received the amount so credited on his account, and are therefore not allowed to say the money had never been received, or unless they can clearly show the entry was made in mistake. No entry or writing of any sort is permitted to be made in the pass-book by the customer, or by any other than the banker.

15. It has sometimes been contended that the notes and monies deposited in banks by private parties, continue to be their property, and are really as much a portion of their money as that which they have in their till or their pockets, the place where it is kept only being different, but except in this respect, the money which they have lodged in the bank and that which they have

out of the bank is said to be, to all intents and purposes, identical.

But though specious, this opinion is entirely fallacious; the money has been deposited in a bank for banking purposes, the depositor has had credit with the bank for the amount paid in, and which he is entitled to withdraw at any time, in one or several sums, but everybody knows that the right to a thing is not the thing tself, but something else.

16. There is a wide difference between private banks of deposit, who do not issue notes, and banks of issue. It is undoubtedly the duty of Government to see that parties to whom it has delegated the important privilege to issue bank notes, or what is the same thing, paper-money, have some solid basis to rest upon, but it is no part of its duty to enquire into the nature of the security that a non-issuing bank may give to its customers who may transact business with it; such business does not require any legislative measures to regulate it, for the act of depositing money in a bank is a voluntary one on the part of the depositor, and is an act of faith or confidence in the honour and integrity of the parties with whom he leaves his money. Whereas it may, and often does happen, that when a country bank note is tendered in payment, no other description of money being readily obtainable, the party is compelled to receive it or to go without.

17. Legislating for banks, in order to protect the customers being depositors in banks, is entirely out of place, for it is beyond doubt that much of the success of the private banks of London has arisen from the circumstance that the Government has seldom or ever interfered with their business; a fact which ought to be strongly impressed on the minds of those who fancy that legislation can be applied with profit to the arrangement of transactions of every-day life between individuals.

It is inconsistent to couple Acts of Parliament regulating the paper currency of Great Britain with other Acts relating to simple banking, which are not only distinct in their general principles, but which have really no sort of connexion; and by allowing the two subjects to be treated on in the same Acts of Parliament, a constant confusion is kept up in the public mind, and a common feeling is perpetuated, that the sound management of the one depends on the good faith preserved in the management of the other—a confusion which leads to erroneous impressions, and which is calculated to do more harm than good.

CHAPTER V.

ON THE LAWS AND CUSTOMS RELATING TO BANKERS'
CHEQUES, WITH AN ACCOUNT OF THE CLEARING
HOUSE, AND NATURE OF THE BUSINESS CARRIED
ON THERE.

1. *Legal attributes of Cheques on Bankers, and the important part they play in our commercial operations.*

2. *When Cheques should be presented for payment, to give a legal right to recover the amount if dishonoured.*

3. *How Cheques ought to be drawn.*

4. *As to the Address.*

5. *As to the day and date of a Cheque.*

6. *As to the Amount stated on the Cheque.*

7. *As to making the Cheque payable.*

8. *A Cheque must bear the drawer's name.*

9. *On the stamping of Cheques.*

10. *On crossing Cheques, legality of.*

11. *On cancelling Cheques in error.*

12. *Custom among Bankers of marking Cheques for payment.*

13. *On the nature of the business of the Clearing House.*

14. *On the Country Clearing.*

15. *Rules and regulations of the Country Clearing.*

16, *Opinion of Counsel as to the legality of passing Cheques drawn on Country Bankers through the London Clearing House.*

1. As nearly the whole of the money paid into a bank is withdrawn through the medium of cheques, we feel that this little work would be incomplete unless we took notice of some of the legal points connected with them.

A cheque on a banker is as negotiable as a bank note, of the nature of which it somewhat partakes.

In case of default of payment, the party presenting it

may maintain an action against the drawer or party paying it to him, on the consideration of transfer, unless it was expressly agreed, at the time of the transfer, that the assignee should take the instrument assigned as payment, and run the risk of its being paid, or that he has not used due diligence in presenting the cheque for payment.

2. As to the precise time a cheque should be presented for payment, after it has been paid away, there is some degree of uncertainty. It may, however, be collected from the numerous cases that have been decided, that a cheque on a banker or a cash note payable on demand, if given in the place where it is made payable, ought to be presented the same day it is received, or at least early the following morning, unless prevented by distance or some inevitable cause or accident.

In point of law there is no other settled rule than that the presentment must be made within a reasonable time, which, as observed by an eminent judge, " must be accommodated to other business and affairs of life; the party receiving a cheque is not bound to neglect every other transaction in order to present a cheque the same day he receives it."

3. No precise form of words is essential, but an order to pay a sum of money will suffice if the following points are observed:

1. That the order be directed to the bankers by their proper or usual style and firm.
2. That it be dated, and the name of the place where the cheque is drawn be inserted therein.
3. That the sum to be paid, which must not be less than twenty shillings, be legibly written thereon.
4. That it be made payable to bearer on demand or to order.
5. That it be signed by the party drawing it.

4. *As to the Address.*

A cheque being in fact an open letter of request, must, it is obvious, to be operative, bear upon it the name and address of the party who is requested to pay it, as well to indicate to the bearer where to present it for payment, as to show who it is that is called upon to cash the order.

2 §

On the same grounds that a bill of exchange must have an address, according to the custom and usage of merchants, a cheque ought to have one.

5. *As to the day of the date of a cheque.*

The day mentioned must be the day on which it is drawn. The cheque must not be post-dated; it must not bear date on a day after that on which it was issued under a penalty of £100 by the drawer, £20 by a person knowingly taking it, and the banker knowingly paying it £100; the latter is not to be allowed it in account against the person by whom or for whom it was drawn, or against any person claiming under them respectively.

6. *As to the amount stated in the cheque.*

To prevent mistakes, and to render frauds more difficult, the sum should be twice stated; once in words, and a second time in figures with £ *s. d.*, which should be adopted on all occasions; for the money in England is expressed in pounds, shillings, pence, and farthings; accordingly £ *s. d.* is taken in law to mean English money.

A banker cannot discharge himelf from liability on a customer's cheque by tendering payment in any other money than English current money, or in any other form, denomination, or quantity of each, than such as a tender for the payment of a debt may legally be made in.

Although in the drawing of cheques the word sterling, which means current money, is now usually omitted, yet cheques will not be intended to mean any other than current money, and if the sum in the body of the cheque differs from the sum in the margin, the sum in the body of the cheque is the sum the banker ought to pay.

Care should be taken in drawing cheques to begin the sum in writing as near to the left hand of the document as possible, and the figures close to the letter £; the non-observance of this rule has been a source of great loss to bankers. For example, a customer left with his wife a blank cheque, which she filled up with the words *fifty-two pounds two shillings*, beginning the word *fifty* with a small letter in the middle of the line; the figures 52·2 were also placed at a considerable distance to the right of the letter £. Before the party, to whom it was paid, presented it to the bankers, he inserted the words *three hundred* before the *fifty*, and the figure 3 between the printed £ and the figures 52·2; so that it then appeared to be a cheque for £352 2s. It was presented, and the banker paid it.

7. *A cheque is usually made payable to a person named, or bearer.*

By the universal custom as regards bankers' cheques a name is inserted as of a person in whose favour the cheque is drawn, and the convenience of this is obvious; for by inserting the name and then adding "or bearer," either the payee in person or any one to whom he may deliver the cheque is competent to receive the cash for it.*

As there is no privity between the bearer of a cheque and the banker on whom it is drawn, the former being merely the hand into which the banker is directed by the drawer to pay the debt which the banker owes to him (the drawer), and the order of the drawer cannot make the banker debtor to the bearer; of course the bearer cannot sue the banker for non-payment, unless in the unusual case of the banker's accepting the instrument.

8. *A cheque must bear the drawer's name.*

It is not imperative on the drawer to affix his signature at the foot of the document; if the name appears on any part of the cheque so as to show who it is that orders the payment, that will be sufficient to authorise the bankers to pay it, provided the hand-writing be that of their customer of the name stated; for the object of requiring the signature will be thus attained.

9. All drafts or orders for the payment of any sum of money to the bearer on demand, drawn on a banker or on any person acting as a banker, is chargeable with and liable to a stamp duty of one penny for every such draft or order.

10. The crossing of cheques is now to be deemed a material part of the instrument.

The lawful holder of an uncrossed cheque, or one crossed "and company," may add the name of a banker.

Persons obliterating the crossing on a cheque for the purpose of fraud to be guilty of felony.

Bankers are not to be responsible for paying a cheque which does not plainly appear to have been crossed or altered.

11. When a cheque is dishonoured it is "returned" in

* When payable to A B, or order, it must be endorsed by A B.

the technical phrase with "no effects," or some words to the same effect written upon it, and this is the import of the word "returned," as understood among bankers and traders.

When a cheque has been cancelled * by mistake it is usual to write on it "cancelled by mistake," and this is considered to amount to a refusal to pay.

When a bill of exchange is cancelled by mistake it operates under certain circumstances very injuriously, especially in the case of foreign bills. For example, a bill drawn from Paris on a house in London was presented at a bankers in the city, and "cancelled by mistake." On the discovery of the mistake, which was almost immediately done, the words "cancelled by mistake" were written at the bottom of the bill, with the initials of the clerk who cancelled it, and in addition the words "no effects."

The protest not only gave a copy of the bill, but also the words "cancelled by mistake, no effects," and a fac-simile of the manner in which it was cancelled.

On the bill and protest arriving in Paris the house there refused to take it back, on the plea that the law of France is, that when a bill is cancelled—no matter under what circumstances—it ceases to possess any of the necessary attributes to enable a party to recover the amount from any drawer or endorser, but is treated as so much waste paper.

12. There is a custom among the City bankers that when cheques are paid in too late for the clearing of the day, to send a clerk round to the several bankers on whom they are drawn to be marked. This marking of a cheque is held to be as binding on the banker as his acceptance of a bill would be; for it is an admission of assets rendering the banker liable to pay, and is the same as if the banker had written on the cheque "We will pay this to-morrow in the clearing."

---

* Cancellæ are lattice work, by which the chancels being formerly parted from the body of the church, they took their names from thence. Hence too the Court of Chancery and the Lord Chancellor borrowed their names, that court being enclosed with open work of that kind, and so to cancel a writing is to cross it out with a pen, which naturally makes something like the figure of a lattice. (Pegge's 'Anonymiana,' p. 6.)

13. It is necessary that our readers should know something about the clearing before they can comprehend what is meant by the above answer.

It has been a long-established custom for the City Bankers to rent a house near the Post Office in Lombard Street, which is called the "Clearing House;" to this house the bankers daily send all bills of exchange, which may be due on that day, as well as all cheques which have been paid in since the clearing of the preceding day; every banker who attends the house, and who is usually styled a "Clearing Banker," is provided with a desk, on which his name is affixed.

The clerk who conducts the clearing business takes to the clearing-house the securities before referred to, after they have been charged against him, and deposits them with the several clearing clerks of the bankers on whom the cheques are drawn; and in case of bills, with whom they are made payable.

At a particular time of the day (which is exactly 4 o'clock) the clearing-house doors are closed, so that after that hour there is no admittance, and consequently no more cheques or bills can be brought in. As a means of ascertaining by whom the cheques have been deposited by any particular banker, the name of the firm so depositing them is previously written across each cheque.

This was the origin of crossing cheques, and the practice has ever since been adopted by the parties who issue them, as security against fraudulent misappropriation. In the case of bills of exchange, they are receipted on the back with the name of the banker to whom they belong.

The clerk in attendance enters the several bills and cheques deposited with him, and credits the respective accounts of the several bankers whose names are written across the cheques or endorsed, as receipted on the back of the bills. He then sends them to his banking house by a clerk in waiting, for the purpose of ascertaining whether they are to be paid; if none of them are returned to him, he concludes they are all correct.

The same clerk having previously in like manner disposed of such bills and cheques on the other bankers as his house held, and for which he debited the several

bankers previous to depositing them in their separate
drawers, he balances each banker's account, and sub-
mits the same to the general superintendent of the
clearing-house (an official specially appointed by the
body of bankers) for examination and approval; and this
is done by all of them.

Of late years the manner of adjusting the balances
has been altered. Hitherto it was the custom to pay
bank notes for sums above fifty pounds, and when
under that amount, it was carried to the next day's
account.

Now, however, all the clearing bankers have accounts
opened with the Bank of England, and those bankers
that are debtors to the clearing (that is, when the claims
on them exceed those they have on other bankers) fill up
and sign an order on the bank, requesting that their
account may be *debited* for the amount so due by them,
and credited to "the general clearing-house settlement
account."

The order is signed by an authorised person, and
countersigned by the superintendent of the clearing-
house. In like manner those who are creditors in the
clearing give an order similarly signed, requesting the
bank to credit their account with the amount due to them
in the clearing.

This arrangement is not only a great improvement,
but a vast accommodation to all parties. It economises
bank notes to the amount of many millions in the course
of the year; is a check against any irregularity in that
department; besides avoiding the risk attendant upon
the carrying about large sums of money, particularly
during the dark winter evenings.

In order to show to what extent the use of bank
notes has been economised, through the operations in the
clearing-house, it is only necessary to state that the
amount of cheques and bills settled at the clearing-house
during the year 1857 was £1,900,000,000, and all this
was effected without the use or employment of a single
bank-note or sovereign.

It is gratifying to perceive that by the mutual co-
operation of the three great banking interests, all pre-
judices entertained by the private bankers have been
removed, and that the Bank of England has also relin-

quished those stringent measures which they adopted on the first introduction of joint-stock banks.

14. Within the last few months the country bankers have agreed among themselves to adopt the advantages of the London clearing, as far as relates to the cheques issued and payable in the country. The manner of effecting this is that each country banker daily sends to its London banker the cheques on other local banks received by them from their customers, instead of forwarding them, as heretofore, separately to the various banks on whom they were drawn.

For example: Gurney's, of Norwich, receive twenty cheques drawn on twenty different country banks; these cheques are now remitted to Barclay's, who send them to the clearing-house, where they are deposited in the drawers of the various banks who transact the London agency business of the parties to whom the cheques are addressed.

Instead of Barclay's getting credit for them at once, as they would in the case of London cheques, they are forwarded by the London agent, by the same night's post, to the banker on whom they are drawn, and if found correct, the country bankers advise their London agent that they have credited their account with the same. The amount is accordingly allowed to Barclay's in the next day's clearing, who, in their turn, inform Gurney's, of Norwich, that they have credited them for the same.

Should any cheque so sent not be correct, it is forwarded without delay to the bankers whose name appears across the cheque.

The following are the rules for the regulation of the country clearing:

15. (1) A clearing to be held in the middle of each day for the interchange, among the London bankers, of cheques on their correspondents in the country, placed in their hands for collection.

(2) Each London banker to remit for collection to his country correspondent the cheques drawn upon them, saying—"Please say if we may debit you £   for cheques enclosed."

(3) Country bankers wishing to avail themselves of this clearing, to remit their country cheques to their

own London agent, to stamp across them their name and address, and that of their London agent.

(4) Any country banker not intending to pay a cheque sent to him for collection, to return it direct to the country bank, if any, whose name and address is stamped across it.

(5) Each country bank to write by return of post to its London agent in reply—"We credit you £   for cheques forwarded to us for collection in yours of
      ;" adding, in case of non-payment of any such cheques—"having deducted £   for cheques returned to Messrs.   , at
and £   returned to Messrs.

Many of the country bankers objected to this arrangement; among others, on the following grounds:

1. That it would place them in a less clear position as respects mutual liability while the cheques are *in transitu*, inasmuch as each cheque will have to pass through the hands of four different parties, and grave questions as to liability may arise in the event of the failure of any London agent.

2. Increased publicity would be given to the names of the customers of each country bank, involving the possibility of attempts to remove country accounts to London.

16. In order to prevent, as far as possible, the country bankers incurring any responsibility by adopting the clearing system, in the event of cheques being returned dishonoured, a case was laid before Sir Fitzroy Kelly, James Wilde, and J. B. Braithwaite.

As the opinion is an echo of the case, we give all its salient points, avoiding needless repetitions:

"The rule is well settled that the holder of a cheque may present it at any time, during banking-hours, the day after he has received it; and we apprehend it to be clear that, where the holder and the bankers on whom the cheque is drawn reside in different places, a cheque *posted* the day after it is received, to the bankers on whom it is drawn, would be considered in point of law as presented in due time, though not in fact actually delivered to such bankers on that day. , In cases so circumstanced, the act of forwarding the cheque by the *general post* is, as regards the question of time, equivalent to presentation.

"But as regards banks situated at such a distance from London as not to admit of the cheques transmitted by them *to* the proposed clearing-house being posted *from London* to the banks upon which they are drawn on the next day after such cheques are first received by the transmitting bank, we are of opinion they could not avail themselves of the proposed arrangement without the risk of being made liable to the losses which may arise from non-payment of such cheques on their presentation or transmission after the time limited by law.

"This difficulty may be got over by giving to each of their customers distinct notice of the course of business adopted for the presentation of country cheques through the medium of the proposed clearing-house.

"This notice may probably be most conveniently given as mentioned in the case; but we do not think it would be sufficient to state upon the cheques" (qy. notice) "that they are presentable through the clearing-house, unless it were proved that the customers signing such cheques" (qy. paying in such cheques) "clearly understood the course of business adopted at the clearing-house.

"We do not think the proposed establishment of the clearing-house can create a usage, binding on parties not cognizant of it, at variance with the existing law."

(Signed)   "FITZROY KELLY.
"JAMES WILDE.
"J. B. BRAITHWAITE."

CHAPTER VI.

ON THE LAWS AND REGULATIONS OF BANKS OF ISSUE.

1. *Country Bankers distinguish the provident from the improvident trader.*

2. *Definition of Prudent Banking.*

3. *Difference between discounting Bills and loaning money by Bankers.*

4. *Difference between Country Bank Notes and Bank of England Notes.*

5. *A Bank of Issue may re-issue its Notes if not above £100.*

6. *When Banks of Issue lose the privilege of issuing Notes.*

7. *As to Lost Notes.*

8. *When a holder of Country Notes may have a set-off in case of the failure of the Bank.*

9. *Difference in practice between London and Country Banks in paying away Notes.*

10. *Bankers may compound for the stamp duty.*

11. *No new Bank of Issue can legally be established.*

12. *Banks of Issue to furnish weekly accounts of their circulation, and how the truth of such accounts is to be tested.*

13. *All Bankers issuing Notes must take out an Annual Licence.*

14. *Every Banker in England and Wales must, on the 1st of every January, make a return of the names, addresses, &c., of every member of the firm or company.*

15. *Difference between English, Scotch, and Irish Banks, in respect to the issue of Notes.*

16. *Country Bankers must not pay cheques drawn on them, except in legal currency.*

1. Country bankers possess, from their peculiar position, very superior means of distinguishing the careful from the improvident trader; indeed, it is considered as a regular branch of their professional experience, that

they should appreciate the credit of the various traders within the district of their circulation, and this sort of practical sagacity they cultivate with great assiduity.

While the transactions of country traders are thus surveyed by the banks of their respective districts, those of the country bankers themselves are subject to the review of the London bankers, their correspondents; and these again are in some degree controlled by the Bank of England, which restricts, according to its discretion, the credit with which the bankers are accommodated. A series of checks thus maintained, though far from establishing a complete security against injurious speculations, presents a powerful obstacle to their success.

2. The profits of a bank are principally derived from discounting bills of exchange, representing legitimate commercial operations, and it is to the banker's interest to confine his business, of dealing with the money of his customers, to such description of securities; should he be tempted to advance money on mortgage, he will not only be travelling out of his lawful calling, but add considerably to his embarrassment in the event of any hostile combination or panic. Most of the disastrous failures of bankers may be traced to the neglect of this necessary precaution.

Another cause of the ruin of banks is making large advances to single individuals or firms on unmarketable securities. A banker should never allow his funds to go beyond his reach; that is, in other words, the securities he takes should be such as, in case of need, might readily be converted into cash.

3. There is a distinction between the discounting of bills and loaning of money by bankers; in the latter case, when a loan is advanced on the security of a mortgage, the title-deeds are deposited with the banker to protect him in case the loan is not repaid. Such an operation is usually for a short term, and is styled an "equitable mortgage;" but it is in the nature of a dead loan, for the banker has no right to part with the deeds, because the money advanced must be repaid by the same party who borrowed it.

In the former case the discounting of bills is simply that of buying debts, and the bills the banker buys be-

comes his absolute property, which he can sell again, if
disposed to do so, or retain them till the money which
they severally represent becomes payable.

The operation of discounting by a banker is simply
this—the customer sells to the banker a debt due to him,
represented by a bill of exchange, say for £100, drawn
by him on and accepted by his debtor; and when the
customer hands it over to his banker for sale, he puts his
name at the back of the bill, thereby tacitly promising
that if the acceptor, his debtor, neglects, refuses, or is
unable to pay it at the time stipulated for its discharge,
he will do so. The customer hopes never to hear of it
again, after he has sold it to his banker; and if the latter
thought the acceptor would not pay it he would not have
bought the debt.

4. The laws which regulate the issue of bankers'
notes, whether those of joint-stock banks or private
banks, are different from those which regulate the circulation of the Bank of England notes, notwithstanding
the total amount of their issues has been fixed by Act
of Parliament.

With the London circulation the Bank pay the dividends to the public creditors; their notes are a legal
tender at all places but the fountain from whence they
spring; they can increase the amount of their notes
beyond the fixed limit, to any amount they please, provided they do so in the purchase of gold; whereas country
bankers cannot issue their notes in the purchase of gold
or Government Securities, but must pay for all such pur-
chases in Bank of England notes.

Country bank notes are subject to restrictive laws not
applicable to Bank of England notes; they are not only
legally payable on demand, but payment of them is constantly demanded. A tender of country bank notes, in
discharge of a debt, may be successfully resisted, and
payment in gold or bank notes insisted upon.

5. A bank of issue may re-issue any notes not above
the value of £100 as often as they may think proper;
and should any member of a firm, issuing notes, die or
retire from the banking business, the surviving partners
may continue to issue the prescribed amount of notes;
but in the event of a new formation of the bank, which

does not include a member of the old firm, the privilege of issuing notes will cease.

6. If any bank of issue, not having more than six partners, should increase this number, say to ten, it would lose the privilege of issuing notes. The law having fixed the amount of notes which any given bank may lawfully issue, without, be it observed, requiring the banker to prove his ability to discharge the notes so issued, it does appear a fallacy, that when a banker is desirous of increasing the security to the public, by adding to the number of parties responsible for the due payment of the notes, the law should step in and prevent his doing so—nay, should he attempt to do it, his power of issuing notes would be *ipso facto* at an end.

7. If the half of a note, issued by a country banker, be lost or stolen, payment of the remaining half cannot be insisted upon; but if it can be proved to the satisfaction of the issuer, that the other half of the note has been burnt or otherwise destroyed, the holder will be able to recover the amount.

Country bankers are not liable to an action, if they pay their notes upon presentation with Bank of England notes, but they are liable if they refuse to pay them otherwise than with the notes of another country bank, or if they insist upon paying them by any other than in such money or currency as would constitute a legal tender in discharge of any ordinary debt.

8. It is a settled point of law that a holder of country bank notes has a right to set-off, in an action by the assignee of a bankrupt banker, against him, bank notes taken by him after the bank stopped payment, provided at that time he had no notice of an act of bankruptcy, and that notwithstanding he took them for the very purpose of making them the subject of set-off, and in substance of getting 20s. in the pound upon them.

9. Any one who has watched the ordinary mode of proceeding in a London bank, must have observed the great expedition with which a number of notes are recorded, by entering the first and last numbers and dates of a series, and counting the number delivered.

The abstraction of one note from a bundle would be immediately detected. In case of subsequent loss the description of the note delivered can be ascertained.

This important operation is carried on by a system which enables a clerk to tell off large sums in the time that is taken to make a short entry.

In case of the loss of country bank notes, they can give no description of the particular notes issued by them in payment of a cheque. When they are sent up to London in payment to bankers, they are the occasion of much trouble and too frequently of fraud. Each note has to be examined and recorded separately, and when bundles of notes are delivered, purporting to contain certain sums, abstraction cannot be detected except on detailed examination; when detected no means are afforded of tracing a missing note.

10. BANKS OF ISSUE are allowed to compound for the stamp duties on their notes at the rate of 7s. per cent. per annum, upon the full authorised amount of the circulation; and to include, on the same terms, their bills drawn on London at twenty-one days' date.

11. No NEW BANK can now be formed in any part of the United Kingdom for the issuing of notes.

All banks formed previous to the 6th of May, 1844, lawfully issuing their own notes, under the authority of a licence to that effect, may continue, under certain restrictions, to issue such notes to the average amount fixed by the Commissioners of Stamps, &c.; which amount must not be exceeded.

12. Every banker in England and Wales issuing bank notes, must, on some one day in every week, transmit to the Commissioners of Taxes an account of the notes of such banker in circulation, on every day during the preceding week, and also an account of the average amount in circulation for four weeks, completing each successive period of four weeks, and also the amount of notes which such banker is authorised to issue.

Such account to be verified by the signature of the banker or his chief cashier, and in the case of a joint-stock bank by the managing director or chief cashier of the bank; and if any such banker refuses or neglects to render such account, or shall at any time render a false account, such banker, &c., will be liable to a penalty of £100.

In order to ascertain what amount of notes are in circulation by such issuing banks, each bank must furnish to the said Commissioners a monthly statement of notes in the hands of the public, and if that exceeds the amount such banker is authorised to issue, he is liable to a penalty equal to the amount by which the average monthly circulation shall have been in excess.

To ensure the rendering of true and faithful accounts of the amount of bank notes in circulation, the Commissioners are empowered to inspect the books of every banker issuing notes; and if any banker, or other person keeping any such books, shall upon demand made refuse to produce or permit their inspection, he will be liable to a penalty of £100.

13. Every banker issuing notes must take out an annual licence to authorise the issue of such notes, and must take out a separate licence for every town or place at which he issues notes.

The application for a licence must state the Christian and surname and place of abode of the person to whom the licence is to be granted, and the place and places where the notes are to be issued, and also the name of the firm under which the notes are to be issued.

The amount of duty paid by bankers in the United Kingdom for the privilege of issuing notes during the past year was £30,400.

14. Every banker in England and Wales who is now carrying on, or shall at any future period carry on, the business of a banker, is compelled, on the 1st of January in each year, or within fifteen days thereafter, to make a return of his name, residence, and occupation, or, in the case of a company or partnership, the name, residence, and occupation of every person composing or being a member of such partnership, and also the name of the firm under which such banking company is known, and of every place where such business is carried on; and if any such banker shall omit or refuse to make such return, he shall forfeit and pay the sum of £50.

15. There is a difference between the English, Scotch, and Irish banks in respect to the issue of notes. The former cannot issue notes beyond the fixed amount, irrespective of any amount of gold they may have in their coffers; whereas the latter banks are allowed to issue, over and above their fixed issue, any amount of notes they please, provided only that they possess a corresponding amount of gold.

16. Country banks of issue are not allowed by law to pay cheques in any other manner than in Bank of England notes, gold, or in their own notes ; yet it does sometimes happen, when the amount of their circulation is at the maximum, to give the notes of other banks which may be in their possession, in discharge of the cheque. Of course it is at the option of the party presenting the cheque to receive or reject the notes so tendered.

CHAPTER VII.

ON THE LAWS WHICH GOVERN JOINT-STOCK BANKS.

1. *Every Bank exceeding seven persons must Register.*
2. *On the effects of dividing the Capital of Joint-Stock Banks into Shares of £100 each.*
3. *On the mismanagement of Joint-Stock Banks.*
4. *On the legal consequences of Directors making false statements of the condition of a Bank.*
5. *How Joint-Stock Banks are to be Registered, and consequences of non-registration.*
6. *How Partners in Joint-Stock Banks may be changed.*
7. *Consequences of one Banking Company taking Shares in another.*
8. *Responsibility of Shareholders.*
9. *Bank Prospectus to form the basis of the Contract with the Shareholders.*
10. *On the Limitation of Liability in Banks.*

1. By the 20 & 21 Vict., cap. 49, seven or more persons associated for the purpose of banking may register themselves under this Act as a company, other than a limited company, subject to this condition, that the shares into which the capital of the company is divided shall not be of less amount than one hundred pounds each; but not more than ten persons shall, hereafter, unless registered as a company under this Act, form themselves into a partnership for the purpose of banking, or, if so formed, carry on the business of banking.

2. The clause in the Bank Act of 1844, respecting the division of the capital of a joint-stock bank into £100 shares, is, it will be perceived, still enforced.

This obligation has, without doubt, been one of the great obstacles to the formation of public banks. The most flourishing of the metropolitan banks have a much less denomination of shares; for instance, the London Joint-Stock Bank and the Union Bank have £20 shares with £10 paid up. The London and Westminster is the only unincorporated bank whose shares are £100, and they have only £20 per share paid up, their nominal capital being £5,000,000, of which one fifth, or one million, is paid up.

Of the ninety-six other banks throughout England, only six have £50 and upwards paid up, and in this number is included the Bank of England. Of the eleven joint-stock banks in Ireland, only one, the Bank of Ireland, has £100 shares or stock fully paid up; the others average not quite £20 per share paid up. Of the Scotch banks, five have £100 per share, and the others average a trifle more than £20 per share paid up.

Had these facts been referred to, it is presumed the framers of the Act never would have insisted upon fixing the amount of shares at £100, with one half paid up, for it is manifest that a person of small means wishing to subscribe for two or three shares in a bank would, provided the shares were £20 each, be better able to pay £10 per share, or £30 for three shares, than he would £50 for one share.

Had a lower denomination of shares in banks been permitted, it would have had the effect of increasing their utility, by extending the number of their shareholders, and consequently diffusing over a large body of proprietors the liabilities which the existing law so needlessly tends to narrow.

The humble capitalists of England, who are invariably the authors of panics, ought long ago to have had the opportunity of becoming shareholders in banks, for the greater the interest they are allowed to have in the public institutions of their country, the greater will be their confidence in the general stability of the Government.

Being attached to the present state of things by this powerful tie of interest, they would come within Burke's definition of the political citizens who compose the British public; and would form a "permanent majority, perfectly sound, of the best possible disposition to religion, to the Government, and to the true and undivided interest of their country."

3. Experience has shown the besetting evil of joint-

stock banking companies to be a too great readiness to make advances to directors without proper security; and one of the principal causes of their failure may be traced to the absence, on the part of the manager, of that proper control over the affairs and business of the bank which is so essential to the success of the undertaking.

All deeds of settlement should define the duties of the directors; for, as it is one of great trust and confidence, unless a director is a man whom the community contemplate as deserving of their confidence and esteem, it is not to be expected he can be of much service to a bank, either by his influence or character.

As regards the manager, it is too often the practice to appoint persons whose previous occupations have been of a nature to preclude the possibility of their possessing the slightest knowledge of the important duties they have to perform.

Young men occupying subordinate positions in banks, find themselves suddenly placed in a position, of the responsibilities attached to which they are entirely ignorant. For many purposes, the manager of a bank is looked upon by the law, and is treated, as if he was the only responsible officer of the bank.

It is an undisputed fact, that in some joint-stock banks there has been gross mismanagement, and in others gross ignorance and misconduct, on the part of the directors, which has brought ruin on the banks: yet this does not affect the system; the same results might happen to any corporate body. It only shows that the shareholders, who are partners interested, ought to choose, for directors and managers, men both honest and capable of conducting the business of a bank with prudence and regularity.

4. It has been decided, in a recent case, that if any fraudulent representations are made by directors of the condition of a bank, so as to induce parties to take shares and become partners in the undertaking on proof of such fraudulent representations, such parties were held not to be liable to the public for the consequences resulting from the failure of the bank, notwithstanding their names may have been published in the usual way, and they received dividends.

The right of a party joining a bank as a shareholder to recover damages on the ground of false representations made for the purpose, must not be confounded with the right which a party may have to repudiate the shares he may have taken, and so escape all responsibility as a contributor.

5. All banks formed since the passing of the Act *to regulate Joint-Stock Banks in England* (1844), and the Acts to regulate Joint-Stock Banks in Scotland and Ireland (1845), are to be registered under the 20 & 21 Vict., cap. 49; failing to do so, the following consequences will ensue:

(1) The company shall be incapable of suing either at law or in equity, but not be incapable of being made defendants to a suit either at law or equity.

(2) No dividend shall be paid to any shareholder in such company.

(3) Each director or manager of the company shall, for each day during which the company is in default, incur a penalty of five pounds, and such penalty may be recovered by any person, whether a shareholder or not in the company, and be applied by him to his own use.

Nevertheless such default shall not render the company so being in default illegal, nor subject it to any penalty or disability other than the above.

6. The manner in which a change of partners is effected in a joint-stock bank is this. Proprietors wishing to withdraw their capital from the undertaking, can only do so by selling their shares to other parties at the then market value of the shares; and as the liability of the sellers to the public creditor of the bank continues by law to exist for *three years after they have actually disposed of their shares*, it is to their interest to sell them to parties of undoubted respectability and responsibility, so that the bank shall in no way suffer by the change.

7. The practice adopted by some joint-stock companies of lending a portion of its funds on the collateral security of shares of joint-stock banks is very much to be condemned, as it materially increases the liability of the shareholders. To illustrate this, we will remark, that a metropolitan joint-stock company advanced to a customer £200, receiving as collateral security a deposit of ten shares of a country joint-stock bank fully paid up.

As the loan was not repaid, and as the shares remained in the hands of the company, who had derived no benefit therefrom, the manager wrote to the bank for the dividend; the reply was, that as the shares in question stood in the name of another, no dividend could be paid, unless a regular transfer was made.

This transfer, at the particular request of the manager, was made, and very soon after the country joint-stock bank failed; when, to the surprise of the metropolitan company, they were called upon to pay £10,000, being a small fraction of the liability they had incurred by the transfer of the shares; "and if," so ran the legal missive, "that amount was not immediately paid, a much larger sum would be demanded."

The shares in question were £20 each, and as the holder of only one share was liable for all the debts of the bank, it was thought a cheap bargain to get off by the payment of £10,000; which was ultimately paid, and a legal discharge given.

8. As the law now stands, a shareholder in a company not chartered is responsible for the whole liability of such company, and as the money advanced on the security of the shares was part of the funds of the metropolitan company, each partner became personally responsible for the liabilities of the joint-stock bank; consequently the security in the one case was materially increased, whilst in the other it was considerable diminished.

9. When a joint-stock bank advertises in its prospectus any particular plan of banking operations, or any new phase in banking, such as the *mutual principle*, or division of profits with the customers of the bank, without involving the latter in any partnership liability, or allowing interest on current accounts to the customers of the bank, in order to induce parties to take shares,—such stipulations, unless subsequently rescinded by a majority of shareholders, at a meeting specially appointed for that purpose, must be carried out in all their integrity, or the directors of the bank would be liable to have a Bill in Chancery filed against them for a breach of contract.

LIMITED LIABILITY.

10. Every banking company registered under the Joint-Stock Banking Act, or under any other Act, may be re-registered as a limited company, provided such banking company does not issue notes ; or if the liability is sought to be limited, such limitation will not extend to the notes issued by the bank, but the shareholders will be liable for the whole amount of the issue, in addition to the sum for which they would be liable as shareholders in a limited company.

Every banking company seeking to be registered as a limited company must, previous to obtaining a certificate of registration, with limited liability, give notice that it is intended so to register the same to every person and partnership firm who shall have a banking account with the company, such notice to be given either by delivering the same to such person or firm, or leaving the same personally, or sending it through the post, addressed to the last known place of residence of such person or firm. In case the company shall omit to give the required notice then, as between itself and the person to whom such notice ought to have been sent, the certificate of registration with limited liability will have no operation.

Every bank enrolled under the Limited Liability Act, must, on the 1st day of February and 1st day of August, in every year during which it continues to carry on the business of banking, affix in a conspicuous place in the office of the bank, and in every branch office, a statement to the following effect;

The liability of the shareholders in this bank is limited.

The capital of the bank is £1,000,000, divided into 10,000 shares of one hundred pounds each.

The number of shares issued is 10,000.

Calls to the amount of £20 per share have been made, under which the sum of £180,000 has been received.

The liabilities of the company on 1st January (or July) were—

Notes issued . . .	£	
Deposits not bearing interest	£	
Deposits bearing interest .	£	
Seven-day and other bills .	£	
Total . .	£	

The assets of the bank on that day were—

Government securities .	£	
Bills of exchange . .	£	
Loans on mortgage . .	£	
Other loans . . .	£	
Bank premises . . .	£	
Other securities, exclusive of unpaid calls on shares .	£	
Total . .	£	

CHAPTER VIII.

ON THE LAWS, CUSTOMS, AND PRACTICES OF BANKING IN IRELAND.

1. *Bank of Ireland similar in principle to Bank of England.*
2. *Prohibitions of the Bank of Ireland.*
3. *How to be wound up in case of Insolvency.*
4. *Agents of the Bank of Ireland, regulation respecting.*
5. *Description of the Bank of Ireland, formerly the Parliament House.*
6. *On the legal restrictions in connection with Banking in Ireland.*
7. *Deeds of settlement prevent shareholders interfering with the business of Banks.*
8. *On the Irish Bank Act of* 1845.
9. *Irish Joint-Stock Banks do not publish any statement of their affairs.*

1. The Bank of Ireland, like the Bank of Scotland, was established by Act of Parliament; its capital, like that of the Bank of England, was lent to the Government, and in consideration thereof the bank obtained the exclusive privilege of banking, as far, at least, as to prevent the formation of banks of more than six partners; this part of the Act is repealed, and public banks may now be established in Ireland.

2. The bank is prohibited from discounting bills of exchange at a higher rate than 5 per cent. per annum. The corporation is also prohibited, under certain restrictions, from purchasing lands of the Crown or from lending any

money by way of loan upon anticipation of any branch of the public revenue, under penalty of double the sum lent.

In case any judgment is obtained against the bank by any person, he may take the execution to the officers of the exchequer, who are authorised to deduct the amount of the said judgment from the sum annually paid to the corporation for transacting Government business.

Forging the notes of the Bank of Ireland is made felony without the benefit of clergy.

3. In case of insolvency of the bank, the stock is to be first applied to pay the debts of the corporation; and if not sufficient each member is liable till the whole be paid.

The Bank of Ireland, like the Bank of England, does not allow interest to depositors; and being to a certain extent the Government bankers, they deem it their duty to give every possible facility to the investment in the Government funds, of the savings of the country.

They buy, sell, and transfer public funds, for persons in any part of Ireland, on the same terms as if those parties were personally present in Dublin, and employed a broker to do it. When the dividends become payable in Dublin, they pay them to the proprietors of stock in the most distant parts of Ireland by means of their several branches.

4. All the agents and sub-agents of the Bank of Ireland are furnished with a copy of general instructions, the original of which they sign; these instructions embrace a variety of points of general practice, and are divided into a number of rules under separate heads, distinguishing the duties of the agents, sub-agents, and clerks; they contain besides minute regulations for the safe custody of the bank property generally, the keeping of the accounts, the conduct of the general banking business, and the management of discounts under every variety of circumstances that general rules can embrace. The latter subject, of course, calls for continual advice and instruction, and constantly occupies the attention of the directors in Dublin.

5. Some description of the building of the Bank of

3 §

Ireland, which was formerly the Parliament House, may
not be uninteresting to our readers.

The edifice was erected in 1729, and, notwithstanding
the changes made in it since it was converted into a
bank, the exterior has been but little altered.

The centre portico of this beautiful structure consisted
of one grand colonnade of the Ionic order, occupying
three sides of a court-yard, and resting on a flight of
steps continued entirely round.

The four central columns support a pediment whose
tympanum is ornamented by the Royal Arms, and on its
apex is placed a statue of Hibernia, with one of Fidelity
on her right and of Commerce on her left.

This magnificent centre is connected with the eastern
and western fronts, which almost contend with it in
beauty; by circular screen walls of the height of the
building, enriched with dressed niches and a rusticated
basement. The western front, which is a beautiful portico
of four Ionic columns surmounted by a pediment, pre-
serves an uniformity of style with the centre; but the
eastern one, which was originally the entrance to the
House of Lords, is of a different style, being of the
Corinthian order, and consisting of six columns, crowned
by a pediment, with a plain tympanum, on which stand
three fine statues emblematical of Justice, Fortitude,
and Liberty.

The room in which the Lords met remains to this day,
if we except the substitution of a marble statue of King
George the Third for the throne, in the same state in
which it originally was; the tapestry on the walls representing the Battle of the Boyne is in a perfect state. In
this room, which is a memento of Ireland's departed
parliament, the directors and shareholders hold their
periodical meetings.

The arms and seal of the Bank of Ireland are Hibernia
bearing a crown as a symbol of her independence; an
anchor in her hand to denote the stability of her commerce, with the words Bank of Ireland; and under the
anchor, *bona fide reipublicæ stabilitas*, intimating that the
existence of a people depends upon the faithful discharge
of their public debts.

6. There are various legal restrictions in connection
with banking in Ireland which are not in force in any

other part of the United Kingdom; such restrictions had their origin from the numerous disastrous failures which took place in that country about a century ago.

The following are a few of the disadvantages an Irish Bank has to contend against:

Every mortgage which a banker may effect must be registered one month after the date of its execution. All grants, sales, alienations, and leases of real or leasehold estate, which are made by a banker to his son or grandson, his daughter or grand-daughter, though given for a valuable consideration, are void as against claims on the banker by his creditors.

A banker may assign to his brother, but a father cannot assign to his son even for a valuable consideration, although the creditor, who claims that the assignment shall be void, was not a creditor at the time it was made.

So that by this law a person, while he continues a banker, cannot make a marriage settlement upon a son or daughter, so as to be good against a creditor; in fact, it would appear that such a law, which is still in force, was framed for the purpose of preventing persons from becoming bankers.

Notes, negotiable receipts, or accountable receipts, with any promise or engagement therein contained for the payment of any interest, may not be issued by any banker. All such notes are absolutely void as against a banker's estate.

It is illegal for a banker in Ireland to give any receipt for the deposit of cash in the bank bearing interest. Some joint-stock banks, to avoid the penalties of such a law, give receipts for deposits, and put the conditions for payment of the interest on the back of the receipt, that mode not coming within the meaning of the words "therein contained."

There is another provision affecting Irish bankers which is considered oppressive, viz.: That if a banker fails, and cannot pay the principal of his obligations, he must pay legal interest for them; if he does not pay the principal, he must pay the legal interest.

7. The deeds of partnership of some of the banks of Ireland, contain clauses absolutely prohibiting the shareholders from interfering in any manner whatever with the

business transactions of the bank; it is a system of entire confidence on the part of the shareholders in the directors, whose appointments are permanent.

The directors of most of the banks are paid salaries, like other officers, and are prevented from entering into any other business.

8. The Joint-Stock Bank Act of 1845, fixes the interest to be paid to the Bank of Ireland, in respect to its capital advanced to the Government, appointing the bank sole manager of the public debt of Ireland, and to pay dividends thereon *without expense to Government.*

Bank of England notes are not a legal tender in Ireland, nor, in fact, are any notes. Those banks who claim to issue notes must give notice to the Commissioners of Stamps, &c., who fix the amount each bank is to issue.

Weekly returns are to be made of the amount of the notes of each bank in circulation, and of gold coin held by any banker.

Notes for a less sum than 20s. not legally negotiable in Ireland, and all notes for 20s. and above, and less than £5, to be drawn in accordance with a prescribed form.

No other parties, other than the bankers, are to issue notes payable on demand for less than £5, under a penalty of £20.

All joint-stock banks may sue and be sued in the name of the public officer of the bank.

9. The joint-stock banks of Ireland do not publish any periodical reports of their condition; they call their proprietors together and submit a short statement to the meeting, which sometimes appears in the newspapers, and that is the only means the public have of knowing anything about them.

A bank, however high it may stand in public estimation, which seeks the protection of the Crown, and obtains the important privilege not only of issuing notes payable to bearer on demand, but of securing its members against any liability beyond the amount of its joint stock or fund, ought not to content itself by satisfying the scruples, if any, of its own members when assembled at a meeting, to which the public have no access; but should, for its own sake, annually publish an account of its assets and liabilities, verified by two auditors of known character

and standing, so that the public may be fully satisfied
that the rules and regulations for the efficient management of the affairs of the bank, on which alone depends
the public safety and its own, are strictly complied with
by those entrusted with the direction of its affairs.

CHAPTER IX.

ON THE LAWS, CUSTOMS, AND PRACTICES OF BANKING IN SCOTLAND.

1. *The general provisions of the Law of Scotland in respect to Banking.*
2. *On the Special Law regulating the issue of Notes in Scotland.*
3. *The difference between the English and Scotch Banks.*
4. *Some Account of the Origin of Cash Credits.*
5. *All the Scotch Banks allow interest on Current and Deposit Accounts.*
6. *How Scotch Banks are supported.*
7. *The Exchange Banks of Scotland.*

1. The general provisions of the law of Scotland in respect of banking were, previous to the 8 & 9 Vict. cap. 38, very different to those of England or Ireland, and even the following are still in force:

1. There is no limitation of the number of partners in banks, whether private or joint-stock.
2. The private fortune of every partner is liable for the debts of the bank.
3. Land as well as every other property may be attached for debt.
4. All land in Scotland is registered, so that it is easy for any individual, by referring to the records, to ascertain what landed property is possessed by the partners of a bank, and also whether or not it is encumbered.

The Register Office in Edinburgh is a remnant of the

old established Ecclesiastical Court during the time that
Catholicism was the acknowledged religion of the country.
The clergy of that day were empowered to determine
civil pleas as well as ecclesiastical. The names of all
the parties who refused or neglected to pay the clergy
dues or other debts were registered in an office called
the Register Office, and after a certain number of days
the creditors were empowered to seize either the person
or property of the debtor.

The holders of all unpaid bills that have been duly
protested may at any time, within six months after their
dishonour, produce such bills and protest, when the same
will be registered in the court books, and in six days
from the registration execution may be issued against
the debtor without any further process.

To entitle the holders of dishonoured bills to this
privilege there must be no alteration, interlineation,
erasure, or ambiguity on the face of the bill. Notice of
non-acceptance or non-payment to the parties implicated
on the bill must be strictly attended to.

The bill must be duly protested, and the protest be
extended and recorded : if for non-acceptance, against the
drawer and endorser.

Action on bills of exchange is cut off by limitation in
England and by prescription in Scotland after the lapse
of six years. In the former case an acknowledgment in
writing or a partial payment will interrupt the limitation,
but prescription cannot be so interrupted. It can, however, be interrupted by an action, and after it has run
against the bill, the simple debt may be proved from
other sources.

The Act 7 & 8 Vict., cap. 38, requires the banks in
Scotland to keep a much larger amount of gold in their
coffers than heretofore. This has had the effect of in-
ducing the banks to increase their charges ; for as the
gold yields no interest they found their profits decreased.
To make up for this loss the charges for discount and
advances have been increased.

The Act, however, has not been able to create in the
minds of the people of Scotland a fondness for gold.
Hence, when the amount of the circulation gets beyond
the legal standard, gold is sent from London to Edinburgh, and is quietly locked up in the vaults of the bank,

and when no longer required is returned to London.

Of course this process is a loss to the banks of issue, but still it is in this way a much less loss than if the gold was circulated, and a corresponding amount of their notes withdrawn from circulation.

2. The 8 & 9 Vict., cap. 38, regulates the future issues of notes by the banks in Scotland without distinction, and compels them to make weekly returns to the stamp office of the amount of notes in circulation, and of the gold and silver in hand. Although the Act does not prevent the issue of one pound notes, but only limits the maximum amount of circulating paper, it absolutely confers a monopoly on the existing banks by preventing the formation of any future banks of issue. This is one of its most objectionable points, and the only one that made the law palatable to the banking interest of Scotland.

All banks, except the Bank of Scotland, the Royal Bank of Scotland, and the British Linen Company, must annually, between the 1st and 13th January, send to the stamp office the names of all the shareholders in the bank.

3. The differences between the English and Scotch banks are as follows :

1. The Scotch banks are all joint stock banks. In England there is a mixture of joint stock and private banks.
2. The Scotch banks are nearly all banks of issue. In England there are many both private and joint stock banks that are not banks of issue.
3. The Scotch banks generally have branches. In England most of the private banks and many of the joint stock banks have no branches.
4. The Scotch banks, universally, allow interest on the balance of current accounts—a practice not usually adopted in England, especially in London.
5. The Scotch banks issue notes as low as one pound. In England notes under five pounds are absolutely prohibited.
6. The mode of making advances by way of cash credits is general in Scotland, but very rare in England.

4. Cash credits have been so frequently described as to render any lengthened notice respecting them unnecessary; suffice it to say, that the bank which first opened a cash credit opened it with an individual shopkeeper, who, instead of putting the money he daily received in exchange for his goods into his till, handed it over to the banker, and left his own till with only the change which he could not well do without.

When the tradesman required to make payments, he drew a cheque on the bank, the banker giving in return the notes of the bank. That was the process adopted on their first introduction, when there was only the notes of the one bank and a metallic currency. If we apply the same principle where there are thirty branches, the result would be the same, but the proportion between the parts would vary.

5. The Scotch banks have carried the practice of receiving money at interest to the utmost extent, and the deposit business forms a very important branch of the banking system of Scotland. Deposits for any amount from ten pounds and upwards are received.

The whole or any part of the deposit may be withdrawn at the pleasure of the depositor, without any notice.

Interest is allowed on the deposit from the day it is lodged in the bank until the day it is withdrawn.

The balance of a current account bears interest at the same rate as though it were a permanent deposit.

The system of banking in Scotland is an extension of the provident bank system. Half-yearly or yearly the depositors go to the bank, and add the savings of their labour, with the interest that has accrued from the previous half-year or year, to the principal.

In this way it goes on, without being at all reduced, accumulating till the depositor is able either to buy or build a house, or till he is able to commence business as a master in the line in which he has hitherto been a servant.

6. Almost every individual throughout Scotland, who has by trade or otherwise accumulated capital, becomes a partner in the banking establishment in his immediate neighbourhood, or otherwise interests himself in its success.

This is, in truth, the foundation of the unlimited credit

enjoyed by the Scotch banks; it is the basis of that un-doubting confidence which the public repose in their stability.

In short, it may justly be stated, that the surplus wealth of England has been invested in the national debt, and that of Scotland in their banks.

The safeguard of the Scotch system of banking has been the uniform practice adopted of retaining a large portion of the capital and deposits invested in Government securities, capable of being converted into money at all times and under all circumstances.

This requires a sacrifice, because the rate of interest is small, and, in times of difficulty, the sale involves a loss. The failure of the Western Bank of Scotland was mainly attributed to the total neglect of this necessary precaution. Notwithstanding the above favourable view of Scotch banking, there is a dark side of the picture; it is impossible to shut one's eyes to the lamentable conse-quences which have, within the last few years, resulted from the *bad management*, &c., of some of the banking institutions in Scotland.

Among the most disastrous, if we except the late failure of the Western Bank of Scotland, were the ex-change-banks, institutions peculiar to Scotland, the paternity of which she has no reason to be proud of. Five of these exchange-banks were established in Glasgow and one in Edinburgh; the total amount of their paid up capital and deposits reached nearly £2,000,000.

They were formed for the purpose of lending money on the security of shares in joint-stock companies—de-cidedly one of the worst description of securities for a bank to lend money upon. A manager of one of these banks gives the following description of the one with which he was connected:

"The great majority of depositors were persons in-capable of working—maiden ladies, widows, and orphans, people incapable of making the most of their money for themselves; nay, most of them, either from their sex or their ignorance of business, hardly capable of judging when their money is safe. It is a very great pleasure to me to know that the establishment of exchange com-panies has been of great service to this class of persons. Hundreds, with moderate means, have had their comforts increased, by the increased interest they thus derive from the money, on the produce of which they are obliged to live, and I rejoice to believe that thousands will yet enjoy similar benefits."

This glowing description of the success of the exchange banks was doomed to undergo a complete reverse, *for the whole of them failed.* What amount of capital was returned "to the widows and orphans, and to those who were incapable of knowing when their money was safe," we are unable to tell, but the losses and consequent distress were very great.

It is the custom in Edinburgh to exchange the notes of each bank every Thursday and Saturday, on a plan very similar to that of the London clearing-house, with the exception that the amount of the various balances are settled by the paying or receiving Exchequer bills of £1000 each, and the fractions by bank notes.

The aristocracy both of England and Ireland consider it *infra dig.* to be personally connected with or interested in banks or banking. In Scotland, on the contrary, it is the very reverse; for a few years ago the following noblemen were at the head of the banks in Scotland: Lord Dalhousie, Governor of the Bank of Scotland; Duke of Buccleuch, Governor of the Royal Bank of Scotland; Earl of Roseberry, Governor of the bank called the British Linen Company; Earl of Lauderdale, Governor of the Commercial Bank of Scotland; Duke of Roxburgh, Governor of the National Bank of Scotland, &c.

The situations of the governor and deputy-governor of the chartered banks in Scotland may be said to be purely honorary, although the holders of such positions have an opportunity, if they think fit, to make themselves acquainted with the management of the bank, and to attend all meetings of the directors.

INDEX.

A.

B.

F.

G.

H.

J.

L.

M.